YOUTH DEPARTMENT
KEENE PUBLIC LIBRARY
KEENE, NH 03431

D1305602

ISABELLA'S BED

Sin amor no hay nada

Alison Lester

For my brother Charlie

Houghton Mifflin Company
Boston   1993

258564   5/93   8/2

Whenever we stayed at Grandmother's house,
we always slept in Isabella's bed.
It stood in the attic with all
the other things from South America.

At the foot of the bed was a sandalwood chest
which filled the room with its delicate perfume.
Luis and I loved looking through
the souvenirs from so long ago,
but Grandmother would never join us.

"Too many memories," she'd say.
"Come and help me in the garden."

There Grandmother would show us which weeds to pull,
and how to pinch the tips of the tomato plants.
We often sang as we worked.
One song was so hauntingly sad
that I always asked her to explain it,
and one night at bedtime she finally did.

She told me it was the story of a young singer
who'd lived long ago in the Andean Mountains.
She was married to a handsome miner,
but one day, while prospecting for silver,
he drowned in the wild Crooked River.
Isabella's heart was broken.
With her baby daughter,
she sailed to a faraway country to start a new life.

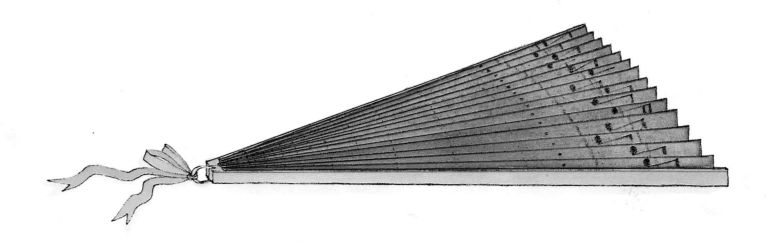

"This was her bed — Isabella's bed," said Grandmother.
"Her young man made those silver pieces on the headboard. After
he died, the center piece disappeared
and was lost forever."

"What happened to Isabella?" I asked.

"It's too late now, Anna," said Grandmother. "Time for sleep."
And quietly humming Isabella's song, she went downstairs.

The silver shapes glinted in the lamplight
and the trees scratched at the window.
Luis and I whispered sleepily to each other
about the mysterious paintings on the wall.
As I drifted into sleep, the picture of the sea
seemed to draw me towards it.

Suddenly I awoke and found our bed
surging through the waves in a vast ocean.
The wind howled through the sails
and salt spray stung our faces.

Flying fish leapt past us
shining like the silver fish
on Isabella's bed.

Then slowly over a desert plain we rolled,
past towering cactus plants.

The sun beat down upon us
blazing like the silver sun
on Isabella's bed.

Silently we drifted across a mirror lake.

The moon reflected in the silken water
shimmering like the silver moon
on Isabella's bed.

We climbed a crumbling mountain road
above a deep ravine.

A condor circled above us
glinting like the silver bird
on Isabella's bed.

Through an ancient city we rode,
in the shadows of giant stone walls.

Flowers hung in the tangled vines
shining like the silver flower
on Isabella's bed.

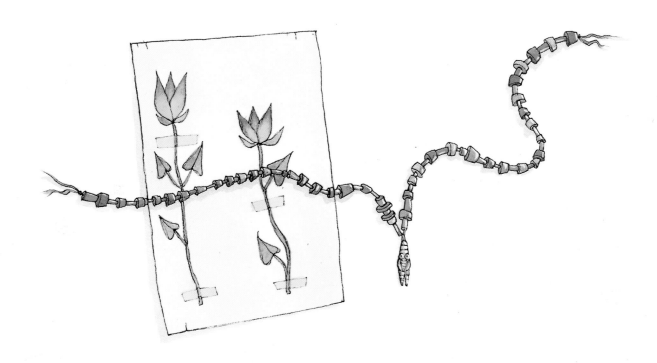

We were swept along a wild and crooked river,
skimming past the lips of whirlpools.

In the overhanging branches slithered a snake
shimmering like the silver snake
on Isabella's bed.

In a quiet backwater, below thundering falls,
we bumped against the roots of a spreading tree.

On its trunk was a deeply carved heart
glowing like the heart on the necklace
that Grandmother always wore.

Then we understood that Grandmother was
the Isabella of the song!
Soaring higher and faster
we spun through starlight
back to her house.

In the morning Grandmother came in to wake us.

"This is *your* bed, isn't it?" I asked.
"And your heart is the missing piece
that you said was lost forever."

Carefully she fixed the heart
in its rightful place on the bed.

"Now, Anna and Luis," she said smiling.
"Let's look through the old chest today . . .

. . . there is so much to tell you."

The Author would like to thank
Roddy for the music, Tibor for his calligraphy,
Penny for the translations into Spanish,
and Rita for her patience.

Copyright © 1991 by Alison Lester
First American edition 1993
Originally published in Australia in 1991
by Oxford University Press

All rights reserved. For information about permission
to reproduce selections from this book, write to
Permissions, Houghton Mifflin Company,
215 Park Avenue South, New York,
New York 10003.

Cataloging-in-Publication Data is available from the
U.S. Library of Congress.

Printed in Hong Kong
10 9 8 7 6 5 4 3 2 1

DEPARTMENT
KEENE PUBLIC LIBRARY
KEENE, NH 03431